ah

From: Aunt Janice and Uncle Gene

Award-Winning Children's Recording Artist
Jim "Mr. Stinky Feet" Cosgrove
HARK!
It's Harold the Angel

Illustrated by
Rob Peters

ASCEND BOOKS
www.ascendbooks.com

Story Copyright © 2020 by Jim Cosgrove

ALL RIGHTS RESERVED. No part of this book may be reproduced or transmitted in any form by any means, electronic or mechanical, including photocopying and recording, or by any information storage and retrieval system, except as may be expressly permitted in writing from the publisher.

Requests for permission should be addressed to: Ascend Books, LLC, Attn: Rights and Permissions Department, 7221 West 79th Street, Suite 206, Overland Park, KS 66204

First Edition
10 9 8 7 6 5 4 3 2 1

ISBN: print book 978-1-7344637-5-0

Library of Congress Control Number: 2020933275

Publisher: Bob Snodgrass
Publication Coordinator: Molly Gore
Sales and Marketing: Lenny Cohen
Editor: Julie Snodgrass
Dust Jacket, Book Design, and Illustrations: Rob Peters

The goal of Ascend Books is to publish quality works. With that goal in mind, we are proud to offer this book to our readers. Please notify the publisher of any erroneous credits or omissions, and corrections will be made to subsequent editions/future printings. Please note, however, that the story, experiences, and the words are those of the author alone.

Printed in Canada

www.ascendbooks.com

"Some angels stand guard while you're asleep.
Some angels help you laugh when you're down.
Some angels are the people we meet every day,
Like your family and friends in your town."

"Rachel's Garden" by Jim Cosgrove

Once upon a time, there was an angel.
His name was Harold.

He was the brightest star in heaven,
but he wouldn't sing a Christmas carol.

When all the choirs of angels
would practice their beautiful songs,
Harold would hide in the corner
because he thought he couldn't sing along.

Then one day God spoke to him
 and said, "Harold, here's a job for you.
Jesus is born in Bethlehem,
 and I want you to spread the news!"

"With all due respect," Harold said, "I just can't carry a tune."

But God told him, "Don't worry. You'll be singing really soon."

Harold felt a burst of joy, And his heart opened wide.

He finally found his will to sing somewhere deep inside.

And practiced while sweeping his cloud.

Hark! It's Harold the Angel

©2003 Hiccup Productions, Inc.